FLY, PIGEON, FLY!

John Henderson & Julia Donaldson
Illustrated by **Thomas Docherty**

LITTLE TIGER PRESS
London

I grew up in Glasgow. My da worked down by the docks, loading and unloading the big ships. Now and then Ma used to take me down to meet Da from work. I loved to see the ships being built and to watch them going up and down the river Clyde. Sometimes I would see an old warship; they were my favourite.

But then Da lost his job. After that he used to hang around the house all day and he always seemed to be in a grumpy mood. As soon as I got back from school he would start snapping at me.

So I took to dawdling home, going roundabout ways and discovering new places. Sometimes I would find myself down by the river. It wasn't so busy as it used to be when Da worked there. A lot of buildings were empty.

One day I discovered an old warehouse. The door had been kicked in, and there was a gap big enough for me to squeeze through.

It was all dark and damp and eerie inside the old warehouse, and I could hear the echo of my footsteps.

I was sitting on a crate eating a sandwich left over from my packed lunch when I heard a soft "Doo doo doo" noise. A wee pigeon was walking up to me. It was too young to fly and it looked half starved. I guessed it must have fallen from its nest through a hole in the roof.

"You come home with me, Percy," I said.
"I'll look after you." I don't know where
the name Percy came from but it felt right.
I carried Percy carefully inside my jacket.

I threw down some crumbs and the
pigeon pecked at them greedily. He wasn't
at all afraid. Next thing I knew he came
right up to me and was pecking at my
sandwich. I reached down and picked him
up. Underneath his fluffy feathers he was
really thin.

When I got home, Ma was hanging out some clothes in the back court. She wasn't too pleased to see Percy.

"You're not bringing him in the house," she said. So I made Percy a box out of some old bits of wood.

Da used to help me make things so I knew how, or I thought I did. When I finished the box I put Percy in it. "Just so no cats get you," I told him.

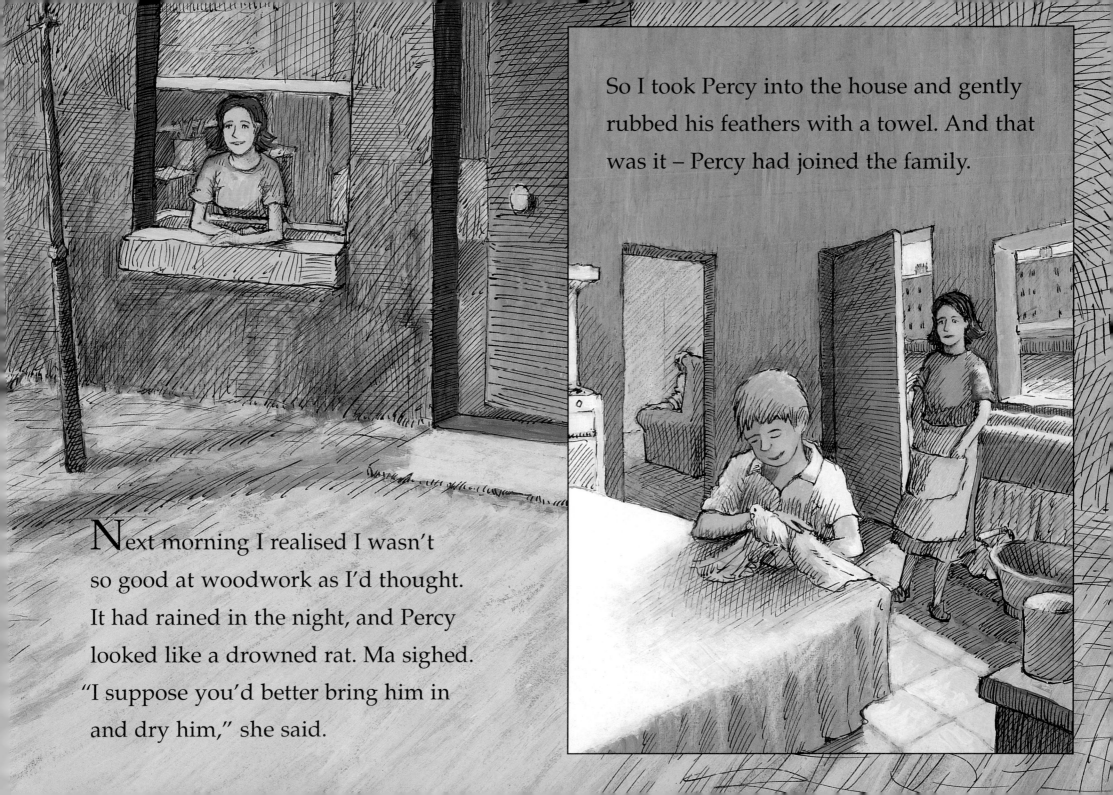

So I took Percy into the house and gently rubbed his feathers with a towel. And that was it – Percy had joined the family.

Next morning I realised I wasn't so good at woodwork as I'd thought. It had rained in the night, and Percy looked like a drowned rat. Ma sighed. "I suppose you'd better bring him in and dry him," she said.

Every day I took Percy out to try to get him to fly. Near our house there was a piece of wasteland on a steep slope, with steps from top to bottom. I would put Percy on the top step and chase him down to the bottom. "Fly, pigeon, fly!" I said.

At last one day he took off and flew – straight across a road. A bus was going past and I thought it had hit him. I ran down to the road and looked around. I couldn't see Percy anywhere. "That's it – I've lost him," I thought.

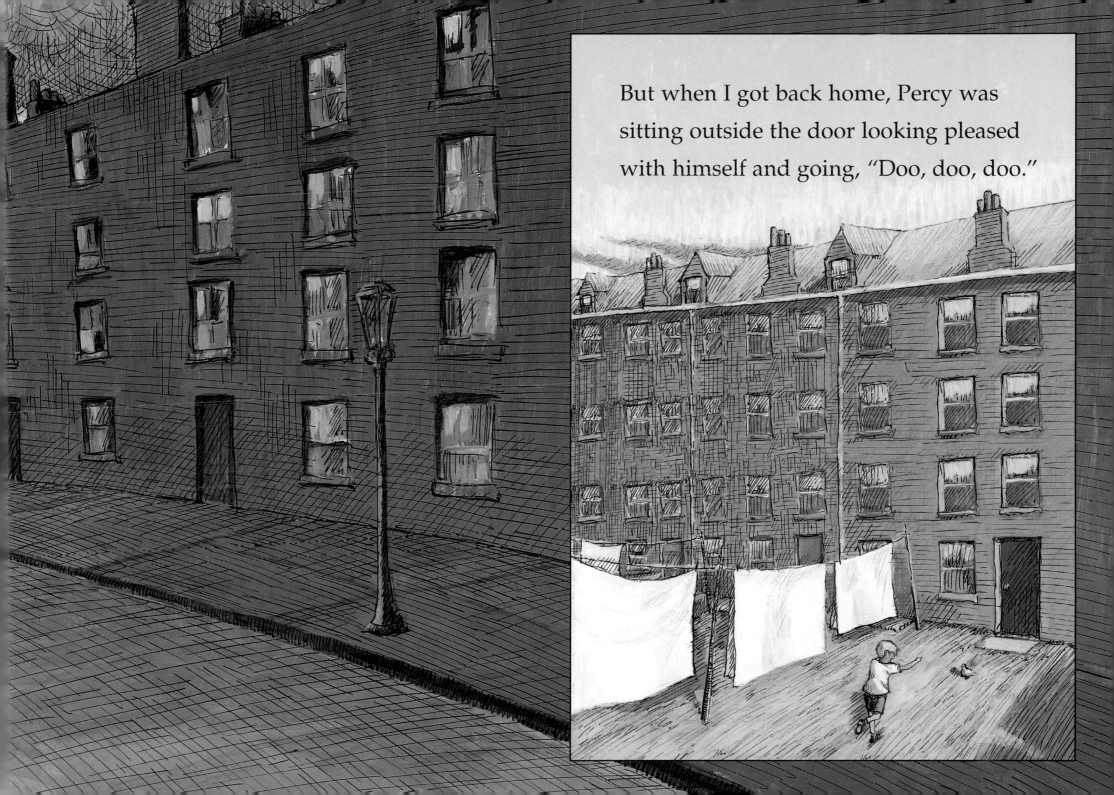

But when I got back home, Percy was sitting outside the door looking pleased with himself and going, "Doo, doo, doo."

I went on taking Percy to the steps, and every day he flew a bit further, but he always came back to the house. He still slept indoors at night, but in the morning I opened the window so that he could fly in and out as he pleased.

When Percy got older he sometimes stayed out all night, but he still came back for his food. Now he was quite a big bird. Da would look at him and shake his head. "That bird ought to be set free," he said. The way I saw it, Percy was free, but Da went on and on about it. "He should be building a nest and raising a family," he said.

Da had a new job at last – it was on a building site in a different part of Glasgow. He wanted to take Percy to his work and set him free. He wouldn't take no for an answer, and in the end I agreed, just to get him off my back. I put Percy into a wee box and said goodbye to him.

But while Da was in the kitchen making his sandwiches I changed my mind.
I opened the box and threw Percy out of the window. I found a stone
which weighed about the same as Percy and put that in the box instead.

All that day I worried about what Da would say when he got home from work. When I heard his key in the door I was so frightened that I took Percy and hid behind the curtain under the old stone sink.

"Where's that wee rascal?" I heard Da ask Ma. I sat there very still. But then I heard something else. Da was laughing.

I crawled out. Da was holding the stone. He looked at me and went on laughing. Ma was laughing too.

After that, Da didn't ask to take Percy again. But he had set me thinking. I realised that Percy would have to go his own way sometime. Maybe in a way it was cruel to keep him.

Our school was going on a trip down the Clyde to a town by the seaside. I decided to take Percy with me and set him free on the beach. I smuggled Percy's wee box into the bag with my packed lunch.

He kept making his soft "Doo doo" noises and I was afraid the teacher would hear him, but she was too busy telling the other children not to lean over the rails.

When we were on the beach and the others were building sandcastles, I ran with the box to the water's edge. I took Percy out and threw him into the air. I felt sad that I wouldn't see him again, and although I was supposed to be setting him free, I whispered, "Fly home, Percy!" Percy circled two or three times, then disappeared out of sight.

I was very quiet on the boat going home, and the teacher wondered if I was sickening for something. When we got back to Glasgow I ran home. There was Percy, sitting on the roof of my house! I called out to him to come down, but he just sat there. Even when I threw down some scraps of food he stayed where he was. Then he took off.

After that day by the seaside I saw Percy less and less often. I would see him twice a week, then once a week, then once a month. He stopped coming in through the window, and he didn't eat any of the food I left out. In the end he stopped coming back at all.

For my birthday, Ma and Da got me a book about birds. It had lots of pictures, and spaces for you to fill in where and when you saw the birds, and how many. Da started taking me out cycling along the canal and we'd see how many different birds we could spot. Sometimes I would see a pigeon and that would set me thinking about Percy.

"Do you miss him?" asked Da.

"Sometimes," I said. "But it's good to think he's out there somewhere.
Maybe it's better for birds to be free."

To my mum and dad,
and to Catherine
– J H

To my mum and dad, who always
gave us paper to draw on
– T D

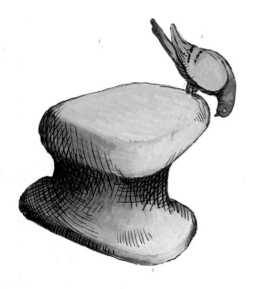

LITTLE TIGER PRESS
An imprint of Magi Publications
1 The Coda Centre, 189 Munster Road,
London SW6 6AW
www.littletigerpress.com

First published in Great Britain 2006
10 9 8 7 6 5 4 3 2 1